ACKNOWLEDGMENTS

This book is a book of poetry, rhyming shorts and rhythmic text. Although this book is mostly a work of fiction, some events are based off life experiences. No names or other identifiable information has been provided. Anything relatable to you might just be speaking to you.

CONTENTS

WINTER

DEDICATION LETTER

To my Great Grandmother, Mary Etta Lomax, the author of the first poems I have ever read.

To my Grandfather, David Lloyd Bills, the one who taught me about not being helpless just because I am a woman.

To my best friend Sade Victoria Shaw, the one who saved me from suicide in the 4th grade, the one who was my friend when I was an outcast, the one who lived fearlessly.

To my cousin Felisha Rollins-Murray, the one who helped me through many dark times, the one who had faith in me even when I made the dumbest decisions.

To my Aunt Michelle Brown-Holcomb, the one who always makes sure I come back to family, the biggest life inspiration, you have been through LIFE! A ray of positivity!

To my rider Stacey Cunningham, the one who really taught me how to get out here and get it. The boss chick before anyone was claiming it.

To my siblings Taleah, Brailyn, Dashawn, Genaya, who have always been my children in a way, I hope this inspires you.

To Jamie, Hannah, Markese, Anita, Cora, Helen, Twilla, Tammy, and anybody else who you know I care for and cares for me! To everyone who has ever supported me.

And lastly to my children Coron and Cionne, the ones who make me strive to be the best human I can be. The ones who force me to never leave the side of love. The ones who I dare to change the world for.

Thank you.

SPRING

SUNFLOWER POEM

From the beginning you feel like I'm something you need
There's something so addicting starting with my seed
With much nurturing and magic I manage to create,
a wonder so beautiful right out and in some ways
right next to the gate.
In my prime I blossom full,
tall I stand
in the direction of the sun I pull.
I transform the beauty of the Sun's shine
so much I take his name for mine
I'm here, towering beauty over most others, my bloom so bright
I guess that's why every time they walk past,
They can't help but to smile on sight.

BEAUTY

You're swarmed with beauty.
You are beautiful.
I mean beautiful like,
like a sunflower in full bloom
on a midsummer afternoon
Beautiful like nature and me being in tune
Beautiful like you've just emerged from a cocoon.
It overruns, it consumes
It seems endless, a heavy monsoon
You are more beautiful than my favorite singers croon
You make me happy like on a workday,
Seeing the clock strike noon
You're magic and mystical like a mythical ruin
My hope is that one day you'll invite me to see that beauty forever,
And off my feet you'll swoon
I am holding on to hope that,
That day comes soon.

SUNFLOWER THEORY

Sunflowers are beautiful in their own right
The only flower awake at night
They command attention
They direct your sight
They resist gravity
They still take flight
The rain tries to weigh them down
They still stand tall with their might
It's like they stand for a cause
Like they stand for what's right
No matter the adversity,
They still pull toward the light

WRITER'S BLOCK

All of the voices in my head are terrifying
The loudest one tells me my desire for you is undying
I need to let you go
I know, and damnit I'm trying
But you see right through my soul as if you were spying
And I'm here, these feelings for you, I'm vying
I tell you I don't want you
You tell me you don't want me
Both of us lying
The constant battle of voices and emotions has me crying
Come to me
It's on your touch that I'm relying
Your kiss has me surviving
These feelings have me going back and forth
My own mind chastising
You say you care
There you go again lying
Of all of this, it's really none of this
It's my unyielding love for you
It speaks to the voices and they're complying
It's that inner conflict,
It has me writing!

SMILE GIRL, IT AIN'T THAT BAD

A smile will shed a light on the world
Even when in your body, pain and passion start to swirl
They have no idea what lies beneath those curls
All they do is tell you to
"smile girl"

FOR CORON AMOR

Dear Love,
You are so anticipated
So hard to find
So complicated to keep
Never stay off my mind
So why do you make my eyes weep?
That is the question I repeat,
Over and over again
I finally come up with an answer
One that is most definitely sensible and true
Love is my dearly beloved
Yes sweetheart, it's you
My unborn child,
Flesh of my flesh
Blood of my blood
Heart of mine heart
Fragments of my soul
The apple of my eye
You are so anticipated
Beyond human's concern
I can't wait to hold you
And give you the same love in return
I only imagine and daydream
Of what your love might feel like
As I lay, I feel your soft kicks
In my womb each night
I pray everyday
You're not, nor will you ever become one of these
Human animal beings,
Who so carelessly mistreat and abuse the word that describes you
4 little letters
Such a simple word and yet is of intricate design
All I ever wanted was to be loved
Not just to be told
But to feel the yearn of one heart for mine
A warmth to have and to hold
'till death do us part

A love that is true
I guess all I ever wanted
Was you

RESTFUL

There was peace in my place last night
For once
Everything was perfect
For once
I relaxed
Let my soul take flight

CITOLEE (CITOWEE)

When I learned about you
I felt sad and blue
I was filled with questions
about what I'd do
I was lost and confused
even though this wasn't technically new
it was scary because all I knew
is that I was always alone
your father becoming a different dude
I had a decision to make
terrifying, wrong, but true
it was just me and your brother
I was afraid to bring you
I knew
it would be another year
another term of torture and many tears
but something inside me said you should stay
I heard it every night while I lie awake
your father had to leave us
just another act of him breaking trust
now I'm in overdrive, trying my best to care for us
that was a lot to go through
but then I had you
I got to see you come out
I got to savor your touch
it was different this time
I knew instantly I loved you so much
you were the perfect piece to my puzzle
you were little but so puffy and sweet to cuddle
my heart softened up, my mood subtle
you were my peace in this crazy storm
you brought so much love and happiness
when you were born
you fixed my heart in places that were torn
I was so surprised when I looked at you and I saw my face
then I saw you smile and saw those dimples in place
I thought I'd be nervous or worried by your arrival

but that wasn't the case
you were and always will be my puddin' boo
Cionne you just don't know how much we needed you
I was just learning to be a mommy to one alone
and then suddenly I was a mommy to 2
I don't think it would've been this way
if it weren't for you
I love you infinity
my little puddin' boo

BLACK AND BEAUTIFUL

Black and beautiful, would you like me to describe?
All you have to do is sit back and feel my vibe.
I'll start by my eyes
which really shouldn't come as a surprise
because they say the eyes, tell no lies.
My beautiful brown eyes say my hello's and my goodbye's.
Then there's my smile that so bright
it gleams and magnifies my beauty
creating a whole new light.
My skin of chocolate descent is coated with browns like a caramel bunny
it may sound funny
but I'm serious
my beautiful brown skin keeps these fellas delirious
my voluptuous curves make cars swerve
whenever I walk by.
You'll gasp and say "oh my"
when you find the shapely softness that I carry behind
it's no wonder why these men won't stay in line
I am so beautiful, and would you look at that
this newfound beauty is so
BLACK

THE POWER OF YOU

I live to love
Loving helps me live
I do not love you
I am not loving
I am not living because I am not loving
I want to love you
I want to live
I cannot live because I cannot breathe
You take my breath away
To make the world stop
All of my sadness takes a backseat to my smile I cannot hide
You
Your face
Somehow your face shows up and my face reacts
I'm smiling so hard I'm embarrassed
That never makes me stop
Because I love seeing you
In my mind I'm loving you
I'm living
Loving you
But I said I do not love you
So I turn my face from you
You know on the other side
I'm still displaying that wide grin
You look at me intently,
I feel the crawling of my skin
Nervousness enters through every pore
But it's when you touch me
My body swells at the core
Kisses on the cheek, soft, sweet,
Innocent they seem, but changes my hearts rhythm to a new beat
Grabbing my hand, our eyes meet
I cannot feel anything that won't lead me straight to defeat
I don't want to love you
A kiss on the cheek
I don't want to love you

Lips and tongue trace a path down my neck
I don't want to
Hands palm my backside like we're about to hit a hardcourt
I don't need to love you
Then you tear away the only life I've ever known
You do not love me
You never have
I was never alive
You say I dreamt of all this
You and your touch
Your scent
Your smile
Your eyes
And your laughter
You say you never gave me this false sense of comfort
But it was enough for me to start loving you
I just can't live
Loving someone like you
Someone with your kind of power

NEW GROWTH

Roses grow out of my head
Sunflowers do too
I've been able to nurture me more
Especially after leaving you
I've been able to discover myself
Learning things about me I never knew
I've rebuked the lies you've said
I only hold what's true
I've managed to do almost everything
You said I could not do

NIGHT TRAVEL

Even in the deepest darkness
Your touch makes my light shine bright
You own the existence of my soul
around the same time each night
You see a reflection of you in me
Close my eyes and easily see
everything we could be
I love the feeling I have when it's just you and me
Take on love in levels higher than the latitude of earth,
why shouldn't we?

A STRANGE FEELING

A strange feeling
the words I use to explain
these thoughts and emotions
taking over my heart and brain
your sexiness drives me insane
your demeanor goes so deep it reaches my cells
deep inside my body you dwell
deeply in love with you I fell
A strange feeling
A strange thing I felt
your mentality makes my body melt
the way you penetrate my mind
makes me want you more, all the time
Your ways of thinking make me wet
we put our thoughts together and the deeper you'd get
A strange feeling
is what I feel for you
because the love we share is so true
and baby
I love you

PERHAPS

Perhaps the love you
keep trying to give
to someone else
was really love
intended for self

AMERICAN BLACK WOMAN

Loving, strong, passionate, erratic
You shock them, they can't breathe, asthmatic
Skin glittering with gold
You break every mold
Every day you wake up
The world shouts, behold!
The greatest truth ever told
The most priceless possession
A culture that can't be sold
A magic wonderland full of grace
They beg at your feet
To be in your space
That hair
Defines gravity
Hides your cares
You ooze sexuality
No matter what you wear
They hate you
Because you dare
To dream, to love, to never stay down there
In the pits of stagnation
They can't figure out why they keep trying to eradicate you
And you go out and build nations
Oh, the things you do when you're focused in concentration
This is history in the making
This is all or none and you're here for the taking
This is your life and you'll live it blatant
They try to get it all
Take your sons, your husbands, your livelihood, your education
Strip you of your pride, your worth, your self-love
Leave you vacant
They must've forgotten who you are
A black woman who will not be shaken

QUEENS WET DREAM

She's a woman of substance, the beauty and the beast, only a king can appreciate what lies beneath.

Quite frankly, when your love is as deep as the ocean
You can't settle for males who have only skinny dipped in a stream
Everything isn't always what it seems
So you run from men who are afraid of puddles
And who take enjoyment in making your thoughts muddled
You deserve more
Even through your rage and your roar
Like a storm about the sea
Sometimes it takes a man with the traits of Poseidon
To calm the waters enough to get next to me
Words written by me for me
I call this my wet dream

YOU- ME

Like sap from the trees
Like flowers that cover the field
Begging for us to see
Like honey from the comb
Thanks to the hard work and dedication of the bees
Like autumn with its multicolored leaves
Like a forest wouldn't be a forest without the trees
You are something I can't live without
You are something I need

NATURE OF GRAVITY

That's their job my dear
to make you shudder with fear
to push your back against the wall
slow you down
make you stall
but you're a sunflower
you know your call
no matter the grounding force
you always bloom tall

PRINCESS, HE'S A FROG

Tried to turn a frog into a prince
but he always missed the vibe
and every time he did some slimy, grimy shit
I acted real surprised
it took a long time of useless determination to change him
to no avail
for me to realize
not every story has a happy ending
some of them shits are real lies

LATE NIGHT WORTH

When it's 2 a.m.
and you're alone
and you think about texting him
thinking of ways to love again
remember how he left you
remember how far
remember who you are

EROTIC ASPHYXIATION PT.1

Drown me in affection
Smother me with kisses
Suffocate me with love
Whatever you do
Take my breath away
Then keep it going
Keep me dying those thousand deaths
Until I am eternally yours

MUSICALLY

Put me on your shoulders
Parade me around the room
Play the chords of my body
While I scream out a beautiful tune

BATTLEFIELD

Die to self every day
they say
How tough that is
when with your mind
the devil plays
you seem stuck
hard to abandon your ways
you pray for a miracle
you beg for your soul to be saved

BIG NEED

In my conflict days
back before I changed my ways
my sisters and I used to always say
ain't nobody blowing down
when auntie Need around!

SUMMER

ONLY SUNFLOWER

You are one of many
Blooming in the field
But no one has the energy you do
The patience you wield
No one has your favor from the sun
Your special reflective beauty you yield

MY RIGHT HAND MAN

Loving embrace
A kiss to my face
Sweet is the taste
My pulse reacts, ready to do this race
You are turning me on
I feel it in that special place
Trying to control it
Be patient
Not be in such haste
Preserve my nectar as none should waste
Here you are now
Hands upon my waist
Undressing my sexuality
Exposing my lace
Moving your hand to please my valley
At an impeccable pace
You've always done it right
That's why you're my ace
You're speeding up now
Making my love juice like paste
I'm grabbing the chair now
Need something to brace
If you were to stop now
My love you'd disgrace
That magic moment is about to happen
So your hand I will grace
You're so good at this
Between my legs should be your common place
Bubbling and rippling over
I shout out to space
You've given me ecstasy again in this place
And just like that I open my eyes
And you're gone without a trace

BEAUTIFUL MAN

I admit I'm a real sucker
for the thick lips of his pucker
for the waves upon his head
or even when he switched it up to dreads
for the broadness of his shoulders
and the baritone of his voice
his delicious skin tone
and the way he handles me when I'm moist
this isn't a competition
he's my only choice
the strength he exudes
when he gives my thickness a hoist
his masculinity in my bed
makes for a quick tucker
I'm telling you there ain't nothing like a black man
he's a bad motherfucker

ALLURE

Like a moth to a flame
Like a child to the light of a fire
My attraction to you
Is an inevitable desire
Like shadows from the candle's glow
Like the hunger I get taking off your clothes
I thoroughly enjoy the look of your natural attire
So please don't feel for the clothes
They aren't required

THE BIG BANG

You look at me
You send chills down my spine
You look into my eyes
I see another world
I see peace inside you
then you put your hand in my curls
You make the feline, feminine energy purr
You wrap your arms around me
You make me feel safe
It's as if God
put heavenly energy
in a confined space
You grab my face
Your lips meet mine
This is our beginning of traveling through space
of controlling the time
You kiss me deeper
Were inside one another
This happens before the action under the covers
You climb on top of me
it feels like when the sun rises upon the earth at morning
Our energies combining
the magic swarming
You penetrate me and I see stars
There's no love quite like ours
You and I create magic under the covers
You and I are cosmic lovers
You are my celestial body
You'll never travel alone again
as long as you've got me

SENSES

You look like you'd drive me wild
like I'd be doing crazy things
You'd leave me senseless
I can't understand where you come from
These feelings you give me
nothing you do clicks
I just can't make sense of it
You smell like happiness
like my favorite flowers in a bottle
like running through sunflower fields
full of bliss
Your touch makes me wish
that I could make home inside of you
use my key whenever we kiss
that keeping you around me
was as easy as clenching my fist
You are so deep in my mind
I think of you and I can taste your name on my lips
I was not equipped
or even fully ready for this
Meeting you I had many walls built
wanted no man to enter my fortress
Funny how when the giant is gentle
those feelings start to shift
To be in your presence
and my mood starts to lift
to hear your voice before sleep comes
makes me relaxed and aides my drift
to take the time for a broken woman
you must really be a gift

QUALIFIED LESSEE

You were never mine
but I owned you
the softness of your lips
the sweetness of your kiss
I've never tasted something so divine
You were never mine
but I owned you
you had a way of making my dreams come true
the masculinity of your body
the feeling you give me so erotic
those brown eyes giving me a trance-like stare
so hypnotic
Baby you were never mine
but believe I owned you
had the power to make that body do what I wanted it to
longing for my touch
every one of them feeling brand new
No, you're not mine
but I still own you
your thoughts, your words, your perceptions
because you believe that me gracing you is your biggest blessing
I'm guessing
you'll never want me to leave
most thoughts of me walking out
nearly impossible to conceive
You were never mine
but I felt like I owned you
and now that you've shown me otherwise
all I'm left with is lessons on what I shouldn't do

PURPLE PROPHET

He was a mercenary under the covers
He was the most expensive of all my lovers
Boy, was he a motherfucker
And sadly I was his sucker
The price I paid was one for the books
I admit I was hypnotized by looks
The smile on his face hid his deceit
I feel like I really didn't have an option
Outside defeat
It's like he could see my desperation
And everything else that lies beneath
I let him in
Against all my beliefs
I let him rob me
I hate I was so naïve
He took damn near everything
He left me nothing
Well I guess he left something
But it was the wrong thing
It wasn't what I wanted
I wanted that good shit he flaunted
I wanted what he lied and said he was
I wanted to save him just because
I wanted to face him when I woke up
Face swollen, and hair in a ball of fuzz
I thought there was magic inside of him
The more we talked the more our future looked real grim
Our light so dim
I nearly lost all my value
My esteem way down
I nearly lost all of my jewels in my crown
Almost all of the trim
Almost burst every hem
Almost lost it all
Because of him

MALE MEDIA WHORE

His thought process is disgusting in public
His words hold no value when they leave those lips
Lips that are normally life speaking
The language of death is now what he's fluent in
Those fingers conduct madness through a keyboard
Fingers that once made bodies play beautiful music
He purposely trashes a beautiful soul
To be able to fit in a perverse shell
Just to appease the peanut gallery
How deep is that hurt that you tap-dance
For those low crumbs they drop for you?

HE LOVES ME, HE LOVES ME NOT

He said I'm the prettiest woman he's seen in a while
I blush and show a big smile
he lets me know I'm cuter in person
he says he knows because he's been lurking
I mean all of these things he was doing
they were working
I would visit him, but he wouldn't sex me
that's for certain
a couple visits in, I feel it again
this intense animalistic attraction between us two
I remember he snapped a picture of me
like he had something to prove
I've never seen him kiss and tell
so I didn't move
I've wanted him for a while now
so it didn't take much to get in the groove
he turned up the pressure
proposed the deed
my reasons to decline were hard to measure
he felt like a need
I decided to put my lips on him
wanted him to know what I truly felt
it took a few times and then he made me melt
then his attitude changed
nothing he was saying was the same
now suddenly he was avoiding getting close
he was avoiding the pain
he couldn't get what he wanted from just me
he needed more than 1 woman
he needed 2 or 3
I went ghost, he went ghost
we no longer speak
months down the line and I still can't believe
how much of a number
this man did on me
how he left my heart back on my sleeve

I can't believe I actually thought he'd love me
I can't believe I let a nigga wearing vans
run game on me

TRANSVERSE EMOTION

Maybe I was just full of love to give
Maybe I just needed to
Give that love to someone
So I tried to give it
To you
To the destructive Capricorn
To the sneaky and curious Cancer
To the cold-hearted Aries
To the poetic but indifferent Pisces
Maybe I should've tried harder
To keep that love for myself

GOLETA

Drunk driving in my home city to the north side
I hope he's home and he forgives me
because its him that I want to ride
I'm chasing that feeling that he left
when he was last by my side
the last time he had me open
love flowing, mood going
I prayed he didn't get lost in the tide
I'm a choosy lover so maybe that's
why he was so surprised
It's been a minute, but can I come through
I want to be with you when you watch the sun rise
want you to tell me again how much
you love the softness of my thighs
want the pleasure of feeling you
deep on the inside
I miss when you'd lay next to me
and play in my hair and tell me
how much you love my brown eyes
I should've believed you when you said
you weren't like these other guys
my heart's still with you they don't even get to try
I'd give anything to give my Purple Pisces
kisses under the moonlight

LANGUAGE ARTS

Pour into me
Fill my pages
Turn me, flip me
My story is captivating
Your attention I took
Use your imagination
Illustrate me
Give me a look
Search for information
Old school, baby
I'm an open book

SEX EDUCTION

(A Rhythmic Fantasy)
I saw him as soon as walked in. My eyes gleaming with sexual sin. His sexy
buttery skin tone had me dazed as I was amazed by his 6ft 2in muscular
frame. Damn I wanted to know his name. Later on, I found out he was my
teacher, and usually would've dreaded the thought, but knowing that this
man would be my guidance made me somewhat hot. His smile spoke to me
in many tones. He sent a chill all over me and through my bones.
It wasn't until our eyes met, that he had me instantly wet. I knew he felt it
too, so I swallowed and said, "can I get to know you?" he smiled that
hundred-watt smile, then we kind of just stared for a while. His intriguing
look made my heart race miles.
He took me by the hand. Right then I knew I was definitely feigning for
this man. He greeted me with a kiss, one that was simple with pure bliss. I
looked around and saw it was just us two, I could tell he noticed also
because he said, "it's just me and you." His beautiful brown eyes taking on a
whole new hue. Then he locked the classroom door, took off his shirt
revealing a body I couldn't ignore. He was going to get these panties and
that was for sure. I watched as he embraced my body, causing an outward
ripple of orgasm, starting from my core. My skirt comes up and my panties
hit the floor. He spreads my legs and my wetness he tastes. He licked every
drop and let none go to waste. Finally, he lifted me, straddled my hips and
glided himself inside. Boy was this sexy man in for a ride.
In the midst of these exotic wishes, we both shared many passionate kisses.
I can't quite explain what I felt as he moved in and out. He was giving me
everything that love making's about. It was fierce but gentle, which was a
plus because his manhood was long. Masculine but sensual, his moans
coming strong. This man's sex was so good it made me want to sing him a
love song.
A little while after he and I finally climaxed. His sexy ass had me feeling so
relaxed. Suddenly the bell rings. I panicked looked around and my bedroom
was the only thing I'd seen. I shook my head and said out loud to myself,
"damn, this was all just a dream!"

LABIUM

Thick, soft, pretty, a beautiful hue
both men and women love to watch you move
they all love the thought of you
many men think of what it would be like
to be touched by you
many people have been touched by you,
when you compliment or when you share your views
when you share your thoughts, when you share good news
when you decide to part and share your truths
They could all go for a peck from you
you're flawed at times and you bear a slight scar
but people seem to still be mesmerized by how you are
you're versatile, you're both sensual and sweet
and you make magic when a match you meet
it's something special when you're colored like fruit
from plums to beets
the color makes your curves seem so neat
you're useful and purposeful but you still look good when you sip
I wonder if it's natural
to feel so in love with a pair of lips

FREAKY EXPECTATIONS (PT. 1)

BODY BEYOND:
Sexy. Not to others' expectations and standards but to mine
everything I appreciate, chocolate skin, brown eyes
but at the same time
it never hurts to open and expand your mind

FOREPLAY TO THE MAXXX:
Kissing deeply
Passionately
In depth with me
Caressing
Touching and rubbing
trying so hard to grasp the loving
Tasting the endless sweetness of my love
Hearing a passionate cry go out
Praising the heavens above

STROKE GAME I ADORE:
The man can hear my body's every call
He knows exactly what it's asking for
He got a stoke game I adore
I'm sick with anticipation
and your body is the cure
Harder and faster, you push through with haste
Stroking so good that by the end of the race
It'll only be my love pouring down in this place
I'll do you and you'll do me
our secret recipe
with a touch of sensual heat

LASTLY, YOU LOVE ME MORE:
More than ever before
You stare at me intensely, as you never have before
you tell me how much you love me
and how much you adore

your sweet passionate kisses
help put out the flame to the sexy whispers and wishes
Until we go at it again
my baby, my lover, my friend
most importantly my man
with you
in love
I am.

FREAKY EXPECTAIONS (PT. 2)

(For me by J. Rock)
What's sexy to me?
The way you sound
The way you talk
The way you look
I probably couldn't handle yo walk
Yo soulful eyes
With a smile so bright
Body so juicy
Game so tight
Yo expectations make my blood pressure rise
Bring yo poems to life when I kiss those thighs
Kiss those lips
Kiss yo spot
Make you drip
Make you hot
Make you mine, reach expectations
With us in bed, who needs vacation?

UNHOOK THE FISH

Last night I dreamt of my purple Pisces
under the full moon
I can't wait for the day my heart
sings a different tune
ready to jump to what it feels like
to be over you
ready for the day I lose the words
to write about you

WHAT THIS WOMAN WANTS

What this woman wants
I want you

EMOTIONALLY
I want you to laugh
I want you to make me laugh
On your behalf.
I want to cry,
And when tears stream down my face
I want you to sigh.
I want your heart
To look for mine every time we part.
I want you to need me
Need me like I needed you from the start.
Want you to love me,
Love me more than you think I love you
And together make this beautiful art.

What this woman wants
I want you

MENTALY
I want you to be mine
Want us to be partners in crime.
Want us to hang on to every word
Want a love so unrealistic and bogus
Even to us it sounds absurd.
Want you to tell me things about myself
I've never heard.
Want to be able to finish what you say
Be safe knowing that with me
Games is a thing you'll never play.
Want to trust that when you're out
Back to me you'll be on your way.
Want to know I'm the only one

Want security in you loving me like we just begun.
Want you to whisper in my ear and tell me things,
Those things that have always made my heart spun.

What this woman wants
I want you

PHYSICALLY
Want you and me to become one
Our hearts beating together like a tribal drum.
Want you to grace my body with your fingers
Watch my body ignite,
Make me fall in love all over again
In just one night.
Kiss me sweetly, gently,
Get my mind right
Stop, then go, brace yourself
Make me put up a fight.
Grab me and grip me
My body your mold,
Finally take me
Make my body explode
Every move so pleasurable
And lo and behold

What this woman wants
This woman wants you
Eternally.
And that's eternally true
I know what I want
And that's eternally you.

IMAGINE

Imagine you and I loving strong
Holding on
Loving deep
2 hearts meet
2 souls collide
A true cosmic vibe
We're part of a lost tribe
Of lovers
We worship our village
Under the covers
Please smother
Me with your love
Give me the energy sent to you
From above
Please put yourself in between
My legs, a passion yet seen
Imagine we had endless time
Imagine if I were yours
And you were mine

FALL

CLOUDS OVER THE SUNFLOWER FIELD

I try to stay bright
especially through cloudy skies
on rainy days
my only hope
left in God
to take the pain away

YEARNING THE STRAY

I wanted you to love me always
I promised you I'd love you in a million ways
every act together was indeed just a play
you aren't ready
that's what you always say
I can't take this anymore
I'm leaving today
It's too easy for you
to be led astray
I know its unexpected
you thought you'd always
have your way
It's cruel
for others' mistakes
you made me pay
It's funny how I am the one who got away
even though it was me in the beginning
begging you to stay

DENIAL OF SELF

It's gotta mean something right?
He stays on the phone with me all night.
He says some pretty mean things,
but he finds a way to make it right.
He says our future is really bright
he just doesn't want to let me out of his sight
even though for days at a time
his soul wanders and takes flight
but he says he loves me
and I'm too far into the tunnel, I can see the light.
Whatever he's feeding me
I'm willing to bite.
He's cheating again
but it was just one night.
He hit me again
but he's sorry
and that's gotta mean something right?

PUBLIC SCHOOL

Do you remember how old you were when you first hated yourself?
Do you remember when ownership of the latest shoes determined wealth?
When you raced the tardy bell to class with such stealth
fearing for the day and the cards you may be dealt
fearful that today you'll be the butt of jokes
nervous about those kids you promised you'd try their smokes.
Confused because you learned something new
something new about you
confused because you never knew you weren't that cute
confused because you found out you were hideous, fat and not cool
but the boys still try to come by after school.
The boys try and try to get you
to be their fool
then after deliberating with friends you eventually do.
Because that one boy said you were his boo
because he said he seen something in you
because he made you feel so much better in being you
because even though you both are too young
he told you that he loved you.
This was real love, it's got to be true
because you know when you felt it
he made you feel brand new.
So you do, you become his fool.
You ask for privacy, you don't know why, you just do.
He says, of course boo, I got you.
As you walk the hallways the next day
you feel like a fool
because he not only told his boys
he told the whole school.
Those dudes were plotting on you.
You weren't the cutest one, but you had your V card
so you held value.
You get home and dial his number
you can't get through.
In public he starts to act brand new.

One random day he slips you a note
that says I'm sorry and I really do love you
You smile and make a sigh of relief,
because you really love him too.
You tell your best friend and she informs you of his new boo.
Your heart drops to the pit of your stomach
you cry enough tears to fill a pool.
You don't understand how he could do this to you.
You never knew this pain before
this is different it's more physical
it feels like someone really hurt you.
Isn't it funny all the things you learn
off curriculum in public school?

CHOOSE

How often do you carefully consider one's intent?
Do you always think about forever,
Or are you cool with a short stint?
Do you care that you may be splitting time?
Or does it not matter because at least time was spent?
Do you feel that every lover you meet is heaven sent?
Do you get tired of your body being lent?
Does it hurt when they never chose to own,
They'd much rather rent?
What level of pain and heartache will make you repent?

DREAMS

I remember when dreams of you were blue
When it was like an endless sky
When thoughts were hopeful
Before the lies
I remember dreams of you
When we were new
They were good
Before you broke my heart in two
And then two again,
You betrayed me my friend
I was never that good at math
You said I was too smart
So that made you laugh
But I knew you were doing multiplication
It's like the pain you caused
Brought you great sensation
How many times, do you think
That from this relationship you vacationed?
For a while I stopped dreaming of you
You started to do all the things you said you wouldn't do
So many other women
Loneliness, the only feeling I knew
Then I started dreaming again
I had new dreams of you
But these dreams were a new hue
These dreams held colors of death, colors of truth
My subconscious giving me clues
Telling me what I should do
I wonder why these dreams
Never helped me to stop loving you.

BITTERSWEET

No matter how bitter the world is
You must always be sweet
That's what they tell you before
They take your soul to eat

CHASING FAMILIARITY (BODY COUNT PT. 1)

Aren't you tired yet?
Being the one he hits up on a late night
promising to love on you and eat it right
and when he gets there and even leaving after he forgets
aren't you tired of your coworkers seeing your somber face?
Asking you how your night was
because, you don't want to tell them you laid the kids down early and wept
you don't want anyone to know you can't stand your place
because every room you enter you can see his face
you can't look at your body the same
because you can only see where his hands have been
you're so lonely you've even tried other men
dabbling in other sins,
you're so stuck on ol' boy that you're using this new nigga as a decoy
you want his touch to match the pathways he took,
make it a perfect trace
you want it to feel just like him
you want familiarity down to the taste
you even want them to smell just like him
any and everything to be able to close your eyes and not see them
you keep it going, taking all these lonely losses
hoping for a win
steady moving, steady loving and it's draining you within
you keep giving it up and telling your friends
"girl they just not him"
Baby girl didn't they tell you loneliness, low self-esteem and depression are
kin?
Now you're even more alone and expressionless
but somehow you still resemble sadness like a twin
You don't want to face the fact that this situation is a bad blend
How much hurt you got to take?
How many mistakes you got to make,
before you let all this drama end
and let your destiny begin?

LIBERATION (BODY COUNT PT. 2)

I'm a bad bitch, I do what I want
Nice titties, thick ass
This body I flaunt
This pussy savage
I'll fuck a nigga, catch no feelings
Cut a nigga off, he still gone want future dealings
You can't tie me down
I'm liberated and free
They can't knock me from the top
If they can't get next to me
I have no wishes for commitment
As soon as you let your guard down with these niggas
You get spent
Have you up late crying, texting wondering where he went
He in the streets making you look bad
You in the hood, head gone, fighting at every event
You in deep, you need a detox like the 40-day lent
You getting fucked for nothing
I'm trying to pay the rent
Could never be me, I'm liberated and free
I will never again let a fuck nigga get next to me
Always starts off so cool when it's I, add you and make a we
Then a few months down the line
You sneaking around heavy online
Trying to cheat with internet bitches so weak
Now I'm sitting here looking dumb
Slowly but surely becoming numb
Still got other niggas on my line telling me "baby you fine"
But the only thing on my mind is how you wasted my time
You lucky I'm not a nigga or yo ass would be beat
I should've never and will never again
Let a fuck nigga get next to me
Dropped his ass found liberation
Now I'm finally free
And I figure why try to tame one nigga when I can have three?

63

I got one nigga he's a dread head college boy
He always brings the weed
He eats pussy like a scholar and supports the liberation, he even fucks when
I bleed
My other nigga he's a little older so he can fuck but he gotta pay a fee
He can't really fuck but he pays so at least I ain't give it up for free
My other nigga he's the goat, he got good dick and he gloats
He don't have a job
But he got a mouthpiece and some hope
He's a hoe, but he got a soft spot for me
I'll comply as long as he supplies that good D and Hennessey
I keep them all in rotation, I may add or subtract
I work out and drink water my pussy intact
Sometimes I gotta switch it up so they can't catch the speed
I don't want none of these fuck niggas getting close to me
Ain't no tears crossing these eyes
Ain't no more looking to the sky
Begging God why
He want a relationship? I'm like why try?
I tried to love before and all he did was deny
Now you can't see my heart no more baby, it shy
I found liberation
Ready to bag a new nigga
He going to send me on vacation
I'm liberated and free
Or maybe I'm just living in fear subconsciously
All I know is I'll do anything and everything to make sure this hurt you
can't see
Because I'll never again let pain get next to me

FOOT ACTION

I will never again help a nigga get on his feet
He'll use those same two
To walk away from you
Now he's standing, smiling at every bitch he meets
It's your face, that messy shit he greets
I'm telling you, I'll never buy a nigga new jays
He'll style on you with a new bitch
You'll be amazed
He'll take her, walk off into the sunset
Leave you hurt and mad as fuck
Hotter than the sun's rays
You're screaming at him
I bought you them new jays!
He gone say, yeah, but she's showing me new ways
That nigga leaving you with no delay
This shit ain't right in no way
People telling you to get over it
Like its okay
I found you, had mercy on you
Pulled you up
You really just going to leave me here? Stuck?
That's your problem baby girl, I don't give a fuck
Oh really? Boy you fucked up.
Because you got a few things, clothes and shoes
But personality still trash, mentality on yuck
One day you won't be the only one not giving a fuck
You haven't learned shit, so again you'll be down on your luck
You'll be walking, searching for me
Stalking
I'm going to be riding by, you'll catch the back of my truck
You're going to yell my name and I'm gone back up
Only to splash your ass and dare you to pull up
Then I'm going to laugh at your ass because your soaked and wet
Then I'm going to ride off in the sunset
Because now it's my turn to not give a fuck

ACRYLICS & GELS

I to get tired of being asked
why are your nails never done?
They never stop asking you, do they?
Perhaps you have a young child
perhaps you like to dig in the earth, enjoy the wild
perhaps you just took them off and are letting your natural nails
breath for a while
perhaps you do patient care
in the medical field
perhaps you like your acrylics too long and it's difficult to ink the new deals
perhaps you play an intensive sport
perhaps you plan on smacking a bitch with no remorse
it should not matter what they say
unless it's in their plan, for your nails they'll pay
your femininity is not defined by your nails
maybe you will go back to the sparkles, lines,
glitter and little seashells
but there's no reason to get so hung up on it
after all its just acrylic and gel

RESTING BITCH FACE

People think my face is made so I can look mean
but the reality is I just don't like to be seen
I don't want anyone to look at me
I'm afraid of what they'll see
I feel like they can still see the tear marks
that have stained my cheeks
I don't want to get super close to anyone
because I feel like I reek
of denial and dilemmas and an unsure heart I can't tweak
I'm not really anti-social when I'm quiet
I just start to cry every time I speak
my heart is still broken, like the pains were just inflicted last week
it was a year ago this month
and I'm still emotionally weak
my soulmate had a baby, that was not born of me
it was 10 years ago they pulled the plug on her
my best friend taken away from me
it was almost 20 years ago
they covered my grandmother, who was my mother,
with a sheet
my heart's had trauma for over 20 years
each incident leaving a bigger leak
sometimes it feels like the bad things in my life
are having a very long streak
so you see
the resting bitch face you hate
is not me being mean
it is truly and undeniably
a part of me

CASTED LINE

Nothing hurt me more lately
then seeing someone I still love
and having to act like they don't exist
It's not that I'm purposely being childish or petty
It's just that our love was never solidified,
his feelings weren't legit
these feelings all built up inside my chest
it sits there, torture my mind can't seem to forget
the yearning and urges to reach out
are sometimes impossible to resist
cutting out my heart and skipping through time
the only things on my list
never to have fallen in love with you
is still my current wish

SERIOUS INQUIRIES

Why must you be in my face?
Why do you lie to me?
Why must you use me up?
Why do you open me up
only to shut me down?
Why is it only late
when you come around?
Why do you embarrass me publicly
then pour your heart out to me privately?
Why do you post me socially
then give others reasons to laugh at the sight of me?
Why do you tell me you love me
when you don't even like me?

TOXIC SHOCK SYSTEM

Real enough to admit I had some toxic traits too
Maybe I just felt justified
because I learned them all from you
But for now, just know my heart is back pure
my words are true
Can we just put the past behind us?
I'm ready for you to come through
Or is there someone else
something else you'd rather do?

LOVE PASSED

Sometimes I want to
Reach out to you
And then I remembered
All the times I begged for you
To just love me
Like you said you'd do

YOUNG FAYE

I wish you appreciated you
I wish they did too
I wish your mother would've loved you
I wish your grandma had more time with you
I wish your father was alive to be here with you
I wish we all knew what really happened to him too
I wish they'd paid more attention to you
I wish they'd taken notice to all the amazing things you'd do
I wish they'd taught you to look people in the eyes
To see the truth
But hell, then maybe you wouldn't have developed your love of shoes
I wish they were nicer to you
You were indeed chunky, but you were still cute
If they really would've known you
They'd know you were quiet among strangers
But really quite the loud laughing goof
I wish you would've made that boy you lost your virginity to, show you
proof
Proof that he really did "love you"
So that you could see through those seemingly infinite amounts of times
People would lie with those words to you
I wish someone would've taught you to love you
I wish they'd shown you at home you were beautiful
That way when people told you
You were or weren't, it wouldn't be so meaningful
I wish he didn't molest you
You were so innocent, already going through a trauma that was brand new
I wish you could've gotten real help then
Instead of carrying that with you
I wish someone cared enough to keep that man away from you
But God was there for you, because something happened
Even though he was family
He seemed to start staying away from you
I wish they cared baby, I really do
I wish that was your first and last encounter with sexual abuse

I wish they cared enough to keep that man from statutorily raping you
I guess they figured that's just what all the youngin's do
They never asked how much that hurt you
They only share and spread the rumors that hurt you
I wish you knew
Knew what to do
I wish someone, something gave you a clue
I often wonder if you knew
That those suicidal attempts would fall through
I still haven't figured out if you regret them either
I haven't figured out if you think living was worth it either
Sometimes I swear it feels like you had a choice between life and death, and
you chose neither
I lost you for a brief time
I've found you but you're still keeping me at a distance
And I don't blame you
I'd probably fuck up in an instant
But I need you to come back eventually
I've learned some things and I've changed some things you'll see
I wish I would've loved you better
I wish I would've chosen people to love you better
But of all my wishes, the one that's got to be
Is when I look at those mahogany eyes in the mirror
You'll sync up and look back at me

CONTRADICTORY

Saw how ugly you could be
Still thought you were beautiful
I know this'll bite me in the ass
People telling me "I told you so"
Saw your bitterness but still thought you were sweet
A sour patch kid, you'd change after we meet
Saw how shallow you were
Still wanted to go deep
How can your conversation be so dry
But you still make me weep?
Exposed me to how broke you were
Still seen you as rich
Still thought your energy was good
Thought your voice had a healing pitch
Still thought you were the man
You just had the traits of a bitch
Further and further with you
I dug myself into a deeper ditch
I like you and I can't stand you
I love and I hate you
I want to get away from you
But I can't resist
I wonder what I'd be doing with my life right now
If my emotions didn't contradict

SMILE GIRL IT AIN'T THAT BAD (PT. 2)
"SINGLE MOTHERS BETTER SMILE"

I get so tired of smiling
I'm tired of the mask
If I had a weaker spirit
I'd be on a corner with a flask
Some days I don't want to smile
Some days my heart weighs heavy like I've run miles
Sometimes I get it together quick
Other times it takes a while
Some days I'm overcome with pain
Most days I'm over life's games
You keep telling me to smile, but today I'm not strong
In fact, its been over two weeks
And I just feel like I don't belong
I only fake this shitty grin
Because I hate when you ask, "what's wrong?"
I get tired of sounding like a broken record
I do not like this song
This constant battle with stress and depression
Got my life feeling like a huge game of ping pong
But black people don't get depression
Black women gotta tighten up
"girl that's just a lesson"
"I know your kids being bad and they daddy ain't helping, but I believe all
children are a blessing"
Well I didn't fucking ask you
You don't know what I'm feeling so don't pretend to
This shit I go through would probably kill you
I traded my life for a relationship that fell through
I gave all my dreams up for a plan I thought was fool proof
Now the nigga who deserted me and his kids
Speaks to me in a manner so uncouth
He only contacts me to remind me that I'm miserable and my dreams will
never come true
Most days I'm asking myself
What am I to do?

Most days I feel so run down and used
All of these emotions, I can never tell the truth
I can never tell anyone I'm in my late 20s with children
Still wishing for my youth
Just like I've never told anyone about
The failed hanging attempts, slitting my wrists or jumping off the roof
So for now I'll listen to all of you
Who seem to know so well what I should do
I'll keep wearing this fake ass smile
Just so you can have a better view

STILL MISS YOU

I have no clue
Why I still miss you
You were never really good to me
You were never really true
I ignored all of the insight,
The hints and cues
I guess maybe you were bored
Had nothing else to do
Yeah your "lil mama" used to trip
But it's just because I loved you
You were shit but,
I do still miss you
I said "loved" as in past tense before
But the truth is
I know I still do

SOME FAMILY

There was always something strange
in the way you looked at me
the way you'd watch me get dressed
how you made your face at me
I should've known a long time ago
that you secretly envied me
your green eyes to my brown
my dark skin to your light
the way my hair curled up
and yours was more laid down
you were constantly comparing crowns
you hated when I came around
still hated even when I held you down
every man you saw me with
you had to have a sample piece
you can't figure out why that never bothered me
why you've never been able to taint my peace
why this imaginary competition you couldn't win
just know that even if I let you in
you would never make it to the end
you still don't hold the key
real women always prevail
and that woman is me

WINTER

MAN & WIFE

Man & Wife
The beginning of life
The start of doing things right
Assumed to be smooth flowing
Such as the flight of a kite
Seen through God's eyes as new light
But, what if a lover's heart is torn
What if bastard children are born?
What if the wife is continuously beat?
So scarred but her smile covers her hurt like a sheet
No one notices because their life looks so neat
No one knows their life has many creases
Like a skirt with a pleat
While the wife cries
They both slowly die
The family isn't the sure
Why the wife wants the relationship no more
The man brings her HIV from a whore
But what happened to man and wife?
What happened to the beginning of life?
Wasn't it supposed to be smooth flowing like a kite?
She looked into his eyes
The look a disturbing disguise
Of what he really felt
Her eyes watered as her heart started to melt
The man she once loved gave her a personal hell
This is one thing she knew she could never tell
So goodbye to this life
So much for man and wife

NOT HUMAN

You couldn't have possibly been human
You breathed air but you weren't living
You had two eyes
But clearly you couldn't see
You seemed to never see all the love
I had for you inside of me
You had a tongue, but I don't believe you could taste
You spent so much time spewing bitter, angry
Hatred all over our space
You used that tongue
To spit vile words in my face
You had a brain
But you never seemed to think
Your acts that were negative and your attitude
Said you needed a shrink
But you played the victim
And said I only wanted to "control how you think"
You had two ears
But I know for sure you couldn't hear
Because I have been continuously screaming for help
These last few years
You never heard the sobs
That went with the tears
You misplaced the silence
That went along with the fear
You had something beating in your chest
But I'm most certain it wasn't a heart
Because only someone with a heart would've considered the pain
Before tearing mine apart

SHARDS

My life is falling apart all around me.
Don't you hear the pieces shatter?
They're falling so astoundingly.

DEPRESSION DAYS

What does my depression look like?
You don't look depressed.
You'll be fine.
Yes.
I guess.
But I digress.
I must ask though.
Have you ever frowned at a rainbow?
Has your favorite store ever been rainbow?
But the thought of visiting made you sick though?
Have you ever craved chocolate and nuts,
and because of your body's new illness you were forced to say no?
You're aging and picking up illnesses that you don't deserve.
Skin is horrible, feeling fatigued and still you can't control your nerves.
When you're out men may look but they sort of swerve.
It may be for other reasons
but you just know it's because of the extra filling on your curves.
How is it that you can't eat what you crave
but still put on so much weight?
Every time you look in the mirror you plan a diet
it always has a changing starting date.
Have you ever hated summer?
Every time the sun shined high you felt it was your bummer.
Because the sun shines light on all of your imperfections
the sun brings all those old memories back to recollection.
Now you're drowning in fear
and guess who's knocking at the door?
Anxiety is here.
You say to quit while you're ahead,
but your mind is telling you that you're better off dead.
And all of this shit sounds stupid and you feel crazy,
so you decide its better left unsaid.
Don't forget the person you were to wed, left you for dead.
That's also a pain going through your head.
So yes.

I suppose.
I'll be fine.
At least that's what I say in my mind
I only desire to feel whole.
Will I ever be normal again?
I would truly like to know.

BLACK EYE

When your lover gives you a black eye
Where does it hurt?
Is it really your eye that hurts?
Is it your head?
It could be the impact of fist to head.
Is it your heart?
Are you torn apart because your lover hit you?
Is it that,
That hurts you?
I imagine maybe anatomy is wrong
And there's an invisible cord that connects the two
Or is it your ego and pride
That hurts you?
Because you know no matter how bad it hurts you
Your lover is sorry
They'll never do it again
And they love you

BUSTED LIP

I don't understand how you could do this
How you could be a grown man
and my face you hit
black my eyes and my lips you split
How could I be a grown woman
and stick around for this
I guess I'm not, but one day maybe
that's my wish
I have to find the strength to leave this
How do you get so mad at me
you just want to ball up your fist
What does it feel like when you see it
What do you feel like when you see the blood drip
When the swelling begins
around the noticeable split
Why do you do damage to lips that you kiss
Why do you hurt the lips you always say you miss
To get into your head
I've always wished
Because I want to know what relief you feel
to keep doing this
I want to know if you feel better
and its only me that feels like shit

BRUISED EGO

Your parents
Your family
Your schools
Your job
They made you feel small
You met me
I showed you that wasn't the case at all
You'd still rather pretend to be tall
You pushed
You lied
You manipulated
You yelled
You were a very broken man behind that shell
You slapped
You punched
You choked
My bruises and heart begin to swell
You've made all our homes feel like jail
You've given me a personal hell
You've given me every reason to go
I'm a fool I still think there's more love left to show
So I don't go
Even though
In my heart I know
True love you'll never show
We drift
We fight
We yell
You've done a few stints in jail
We separate
You still fuck everyone
You have a baby with someone
You barely know
You had a baby with a POF hoe
You've finally found a way to make me go

I think that bruised both our egos

AGONY

I am scared
I'm afraid of the pain
Have you ever feared
that you'd drown in the rain
that's the feeling I get
when I think of loving you again
the feeling of death overtakes me
because I'll never love you the same
in fact, after what you've done
loving you at all
would be insane

NIGHTMARE

You came and were different
You swept me off my feet
You made me feel like cherishing
The things you'd let me keep
I never knew I could love someone so much
Every time you left my side
My soul yearned for your touch
Then we found out about our first seed
I finally admitted that it was you I need
It's like this news made your heart turn cold
I started tracing the stories you gave
Discovering the lies you've told
That loving touch
Turned to blows
The love that was flowing
Was starting to slow
I can't seem to find the man that I know
I birthed your first baby boy
I thought we'd share nothing but joy
But even during labor you were looking for someone else
You showed me there was nothing I could do
There would always be someone else with you
5:58 p.m.
It's time to start pushing him
6:30 p.m.
I've pushed, you separated him
6:56 p.m.
The baby is sick, the NICU took him
7:27 p.m.
You left on a whim
You left me alone again
I had no one there
No family, no friends
You cheated on me the night I had our first baby

You didn't call or check on me or the baby
I've made a lot of excuses
A lot of what if's and maybe's
But the truth is you've never truly viewed me as your lady
And to think
This was just one of the first nightmares you gave me

PAINFUL DAYS

What do you do on the days that your heart screams?

How could you ever love somebody more than you've loved me?

Or when your minds confused,

How could you do this to me?

Because it's not supposed to last between the cheater and the cheatee.

DIAGNOSIS

It's a major pain
Feeling worthless
Feeling like there's nothing to gain
Feeling like life's gone down the drain
Feeling like you've made too many mistakes
Feeling a sadness you can't shake
Feeling the darkness overcome you
Feeling so unsure
unsure about how much more
of the darkness you can take
Feeling like you might find peace
for heaven's sake
If from this meritless body
your soul dissipates

INTERNAL HOPE SEARCH

Maybe I don't really need to have another child to right the wrongs of my
past
Maybe I can still start over with the children I have
I hope to become a much better mother than I am today
I hope to become a much better woman than I am today
I really hope to become a much better human than I am today
I really don't want this disease to be the end all of my happiness
I don't want this to be the focal point of my life either
I want to be happy again
I want to be lighthearted again
Is that even possible?
Will I ever feel happiness or love again?
Will anyone ever love me again?
And if they do, will it be God-sent?
Will I know by how it feels?
Will I have to search for it?
Or will it eventually find me?

NARC WISHING WELL

It really hurts
It burns like hell
You spent all this time
They made life feel like jail
You prayed for kindness and soft words
And all they did was yell
Then they discarded you
Left you with a heart that swells
They've left you for good
And didn't even wish you well

LEAVE ME ALONE

It's best to let sleeping dogs lie
and I'm that bitch
I'll kill you, watch the pain seep out
while staring in your eyes
All you did was hurt me
All you did was lie
All I did was love you
All you did was make me cry
All I wanted was you
You didn't even try
Its best to stay away from me
If you value your life

THE SIGNS

I am too tired to wake up on time
I really don't want to go
If I stayed home, I'm sure no one would notice
If I cover these scars and bruises,
No one would know
because I'm unhappy as hell
and that doesn't seem to show
I told someone about the darkness
Deep in my soul
They gave me a strong look
and continued to talk about the coming snow
I keep trying to be nice to people, to do good things
because I've heard you reap what you sow
maybe there's more to it
I just don't know
My family is having holiday dinner together
I won't go
My house is cluttered
with dirty dishes, trash and soiled clothes
I am too tired to clean
but a full deep cleanse is my goal
No one cares
No one loves me
No one knows
No one loves me
No one cares
Not a single soul
No one see's how much life's taken a toll
No one cares
and if I die today
No one would even know

SUICIDE DAYS

I thought about going through with it today
Was thinking about actually listening
To what my mind has to say
I played the scenes in my mind
Wanted to mentally perfect them
So I kept them on rewind
I don't think there's a will or a way
That can make me want to stay
Pain and heartache is all I can seem to find
Maybe if I come here again
I'll live a life that's mine
Maybe someone will love me and never leave me
Maybe someday
Maybe next time

SUNFLOWER FIELDS

For all the mothers, both single and taken.
For all of the lovers, both happy or just complacent.
For all of the men, unevolved and the awakened.
For all of the love that each soul has forsaken.
For everyone in search of everything good, everything true.
I hope you continue to pull upward,
just as the sunflowers do.
I hope this book calms you, that you may pass your morning "dew"
understand that we all have hurt, pain and other
personal struggles to get through.
So when you're out and about and see any yellow hue,
just know and understand by God we're all connected in the field
and I'm radiating love to every one of you.

ABOUT THE AUTHOR

Corinne is a mother of 2 boys, a lover of learning, an avid reader, a self-proclaimed foodie and a true science nerd who also has an interest in art. She was born and raised in Youngstown, Ohio and moved frequently after leaving. Now settled for the moment she attends Kent State University and is majoring in Nursing with a minor in Public Health. Promoting health among people with health disparities is a strong passion. Our health is more than just healing wounds and nursing colds, it is the synchrony of mind, body and spirit. Protect your health. -Corinne ♥

INSTAGRAM: @nerdysunflowerqueen
FACEBOOK: The Nerdy Sunflower Queen Corinne B
♥TUMBLR: nerdysunflowerqueen